Happy Birthday Tina T. Spoon

button moon

Story and original designs by Ian Allen

Adapted from the Thames Television series featuring the Playboard Puppet Theatre

Puppets and Settings by John Thirtle

HiPPO

Hippo Books
Scholastic Publications Limited
London

Today is Tina's birthday. Mrs Spoon is wishing Tina a Happy Birthday. If she gets washed and dressed quickly and comes downstairs she might just find a present waiting for her. Tina asks if the Postman has been. Mrs Spoon hasn't seen him yet. He's a bit late.

Mr Pot the Postman *has* arrived. He knows it is Tina's birthday because one of the envelopes has an orange sticker saying 'Happy Birthday'. He will give Tina a surprise. He posts the birthday cards under the door of the spaceship and creeps away. Mr Pot doesn't even 'toot-toot' his post van.

Tina is pleased with her birthday present. It is a computer game. She presses the button. Ping-ping-ping! Mrs Spoon thinks everyone else must have forgotten Tina's birthday – even Granny Spoon. Mr Spoon suggests they take off for Button Moon. When they get back the birthday cards may be on the mat.

Tina opens the spaceship door to find a pile of
envelopes on the floor. What a surprise! Mr Pot the
Postman was playing a birthday game. Mrs Spoon
sees a brown envelope. It's the telephone bill – more
of a shock than a surprise! Time to take off for the
birthday flight to Button Moon. 5 . . . 4 . . . 3 . . .
2 . . . 1 . . . Blast off!

Tina likes watching the floating balloons. She has opened her birthday cards. Granny Spoon's card has a pretty flower on the front and a postal order inside. There is a card from Tina's uncle with a puppy on it and a card from her schoolfriends with a picture of a clown. But there's no card from Egbert. He has forgotten!

They land safely on Button Moon. Vacuum Cleaner and Small Bottle are there to meet them. 'Hello Tina, Happy Birthday! Here's your birthday card.' Zzzzzzh. Vacuum Cleaner did have a birthday card for Tina – but he swallowed it.

'Hello there!' Tina recognises that voice. It's Queenie Jelly!

Queenie Jelly is wobbling and shaking. 'Happy Birthday Tina. I'm so excited because ice skating will be taking place on top of the iced cake. It's such a wonderful cake with an ice-capped mountain! The very clever ice skater is Miss Marzy Pan. A fanfare for Marzy please!'

Marzy appears standing on top of the ice-capped
mountain. She slides down the mountain and whirls
and twirls on the ice. Tina thinks she is very clever.
Then, all of a sudden . . . CRAAACK! The ice cracks
and Marzy falls through.

Queenie Jelly is most upset. 'Oh dear, Marzy has fallen through the icing. What are we going to do?' Mrs Spoon comes to the rescue and helps her out.

'Thank you so much Mrs Spoon. The next time Marzy goes ice skating we must make sure the icing has set hard.'

'Jolly good!' cries Queenie Jelly. 'Here is Jam Doughnut.'

'Happy Birthday, Tina. All together now!'

'Three cheers for Tina. Hip Hip Hooray! Hip Hip Hooray! Hip Hip Hooray!'

Rag Doll shouts across Button Moon, 'Over here, Tina – we want to wish you a Happy Birthday!' The Spoon Family can see Rag Doll doing her disco dancing. Freddy Teddy is practising the piano. 'Rag Doll, I wish you'd turn down your stereo. I can't hear myself playing.'

Toffee the Clown says, 'The music is putting me off my juggling – the sweets are going everywhere.'

'Sorry,' says Rag Doll. 'I'll turn the music down and I'll sit here while you play the piano. Oh no! I've sat on a sticky toffee! I can't do my disco dancing with a box stuck to my bottom!'

'I'll unstick you,' says Freddy Teddy. 'There. Why don't we all do disco dancing?' Rag Doll agrees and everyone joins in – even Mr Spoon!

Tina is having a lovely birthday. She waves goodbye to the toys, 'Goodbye!' Mrs Spoon says that before they leave Button Moon there is time to have a look through the telescope. They all look to see what they can find.

Through the telescope they can see Gertie and Bertie. Bertie has brought Gertie breakfast in bed. 'Come on Gertie, you great big snoring lump! Time to get up!'

'Oh Bertie,' replies Gertie. 'I was fast asleep. I was dreaming that you were King and I was Queen. Wouldn't that be nice?' Bertie laughs.

'My love, why don't you wish for your Fairy Godmother?'

'What a good idea, Bertie. I wish my Fairy Godmother was here,' says Gertie. Suddenly there is a flash and a shower of cornflakes. Fairy Mary appears. 'I was fast alseep in the cornflakes!'

Gertie says, 'I'm sorry Fairy Mary. Please may we have three wishes?'

'All right. You can have three wishes,' replies Fairy Mary. 'But they will only last the day as it's the month of May. I must fly, Bye!'

Fairy Mary disappears and Gertie jumps up and down with excitement. 'Whatever's that noise?'

'My love, it's the cornflakes,' says Bertie. 'You're crunching them into the floor.'

'Never mind,' replies Gertie. 'Let's make the wish. I wish Bertie and I could be King and Queen for a day!' The magic works and Bertie and Gertie are wearing the cloaks and crowns.

'Gertie, let's ask to live in a palace. Kings and Queens wouldn't want a bedroom like this.' Gertie agrees, 'My husband and I wish to be in a palace!'

The magic works and Bertie and Gertie find themselves in a palace bedroom. 'Look Bertie, a Royal Bed and Royal Curtains and a Royal Carpet,' says Gertie.

'My love, the cornflakes are in silver bowls. Can we have breakfast?' asks Bertie. Gertie is far too excited. Then two yapping corgi dogs chase into the bedroom.

'Look Bertie – corgis. We must be in Buckingham Palace,' says Gertie. Bertie shakes his head. 'We mustn't let them climb on to the bed. Let's go out onto the balcony.' They gaze down on the traffic in the streets.

Gertie says, 'Bertie, you can see for miles. Don't those guardsmen look smart.' Bertie says, 'Let's go back inside. It's been marvellous being King and Queen for a day.'

Gertie agrees, 'Fairy Mary did say the magic would only last a day.' Suddenly they are back in their own bedroom. Gertie says, 'We had a lovely time – but there's no place like home. I wouldn't wish to live in a palace for all the tea in China.' There is a flash! It's raining tea bags!

Bertie says, 'Oh no, we still had a third wish left and Fairy Mary thought you wished for all the tea in China!'

'Never mind,' replies Gertie. 'Go and put the kettle on!' And they both laugh!

Mrs Spoon puts the telescope back in the spaceship and they all get ready for the countdown. 5 . . . 4 . . . 3 . . . 2 . . . 1 . . . Blast off! Mr Spoon tells Tina they are not going straight home – they are going to fly to Egbert's house. Vanilla has invited them for Tina's birthday tea.

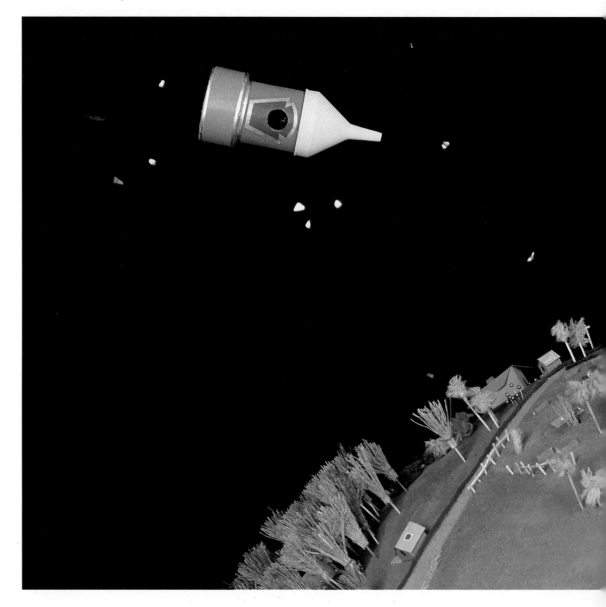

From the spaceship window they can see the tallest block of flats. That is where Egbert lives. Mrs Spoon presses the round button to land the spaceship in the car park.

Egbert gives Tina the birthday card he has made himself. As he gives her the present he bought, he drops it on the floor and it bounces around the room. Tina thinks it must be a ball. They all laugh and Vanilla and Egbert wish Tina a Happy Birthday!